# Tyler the Fish
## and the Lake Erie Bully

### by Meaghan Fisher
### art by Tim Rowe

Gypsy
Publications

Published in 2016, by Gypsy Publications
Troy, OH 45373, U.S.A.
www.GypsyPublications.com

Fisher, Meaghan
*Tyler the Fish and the Lake Erie Bully*
Story by Meaghan Fisher
art by Tim Rowe & Sandra Burns
Tyler the Fish and Lake Erie Series

ISBN 978-1-938768-70-5 (paperback)
ISBN 978-1-938768-69-9 (hardback)

Library of Congress Control Number
2016950001

Edited by Jon Williams
Book Design by Tim Rowe

This book is for everyone...

Sometimes others might mistreat you and hurt your feelings. It is not right to bully others, nor is bullying the answer to anyone's problems! Always try to be kind and loving to others, even when it's not an easy thing to do. If you are being mistreated in any way; make sure to seek an adult to talk to. Plus, never forget...you are important, too!!!

There once was a little bass named Tyler. Tyler lived in one of the great lakes in Ohio called Lake Erie.

Tyler was so excited for his first day of school! His mother had bought him his first backpack and she had packed his lunch. Now she was going to walk him to school to meet his new teacher.

After a short walk, Tyler and his mother
arrived at the door of his new school.
There he saw his best friend, Jimmy.
"Hey, Tyler, are you excited to meet our
teacher?" asked Jimmy.

"Oh, yes," replied Tyler. "I can't wait to meet
our teacher and see our classroom."

"Me too!" exclaimed Jimmy. "I hear that we
have recess where you can go outside and play!"

"Awesome," said Tyler. "Our first recess!"

"Kids, I'm Mrs. Patty," said Tyler and Jimmy's new teacher. "Come with me to your new classroom."

Mrs. Patty led them down the hallway and into their classroom. They saw other little fish sitting on a rug in the middle of the floor for story time. Tyler and Jimmy joined them and enjoyed the story Mrs. Patty read to them. Then it was time for lunch.

Tyler and Jimmy were eating their packed lunches in the school cafeteria and talking about their excitement for recess when a large, mean-looking trout came up to Tyler.

"Give me your lunch, kid!" demanded the trout.
"Why would I give you my lunch?" asked Tyler.
"It's mine. My mother made it for me."

"Give it to me now!" demanded the mean fish,
looking angrier. "Or I'll give you a knuckle sandwich!"
The fish held his fins up at Tyler, and then grabbed
Tyler's lunch sack out of his grasp and swam off.

"Hey!" exclaimed Tyler. "That's my lunch!"
"Don't worry, Tyler," said Jimmy. "You can have some of my lunch."
"Thanks," replied Tyler. "It's nice of you to share."

After school, Tyler went home and told his mother what happened at lunch.

"Tyler," she said, "sometimes there will be fish that may be mean to you or mistreat you. They are called bullies. That fish took your lunch and hurt your feelings, but you wouldn't do something like that to another fish. Right?"

"Right," Tyler told his mother.
"Good." Tyler's mother gave her little fish a hug.

The next day at school, Tyler was sitting with his friend, Jimmy, when the mean trout approached him again. "Give me your lunch, kid!" he shouted at Tyler.

"No," cried Tyler. "It's mine and you can't have it!"
"Are you crazy, kid?" the angry trout yelled at Tyler.
"Just give up and give me your lunch." He grabbed at
Tyler's lunch bag, but Tyler held it close.

"No!" shouted Tyler. "I feel sorry for you because you hurt fishes' feelings. I would never do something like that to another fish because I know it's wrong to hurt others' feelings. We could be friends if you would just be nice."

"Sorry," the trout said with his head down, looking embarrassed. He swam away from Tyler and never bothered him again.

Tyler went home and told his mother what happened at lunch that day.

"Tyler," cried his mother, "I am so proud of you! You stuck up for yourself and explained to that mean fish that what he was doing was wrong. Now he may never do that to another fish again!"

"You're proud of me?" asked Tyler.

"Yes, honey," said Tyler's mother as she wrapped her fins around her son. "Good job!"

Tyler had learned a very important lesson. He learned that it was wrong to hurt others' feelings or take something that didn't belong to you, and that it was important to stick up for what is right, no matter how big or small you might be.

CPSIA information can be obtained at www.ICGtesting.com
Printed in the USA
BVIW12n0114100418
512951BV00005B/23